E. 153.4   Allington, Richard
 All   L   7395

          Thinking

                          $11.97

DATE DUE

E 153.4   Allington, Richard
 All   L
                          7395

          Thinking

                          $11.97

DATE DUE   BORROWER'S NAME

Thinking

Copyright © 1980, Raintree Publishers Inc.

All rights reserved. No part of this book may be
reproduced or utilized in any form or by any means,
electronic or mechanical, including photocopying,
recording, or by any information storage and retrieval
system, without permission in writing from the Publisher.
Inquiries should be addressed to Raintree Childrens Books.
330 East Kilbourn Avenue, Milwaukee, Wisconsin 53202

Library of Congress Number: 80-15390

  4 5 6 7 8 9 0 88 87 86 85

Printed in the United States of America.

Library of Congress Cataloging in Publication Data

Allington, Richard L
  Thinking.

  (Beginning to learn about)
  SUMMARY: Presents situations that illustrate
various thought and problem solving processes, such
as making choices, putting things in order, or
making sense out of things. Includes related
activities.
  1. Thought and thinking — Juvenile literature.
2. Problem solving — Juvenile literature.
[1. Decision making. 2. Problem solving.
3. Thought and thinking] I. Krull, Kathleen,
joint author. II. Garcia, Tom. III. Title.
IV. Series.
BF455.A47   153.4'2   80-15390
ISBN 0-8172-1319-8

Richard L. Allington is Associate Professor, Department of Reading,
State University of New York at Albany.
Kathleen Krull is the author of nineteen books for children.

BEGINNING TO LEARN ABOUT

THINKING

BY RICHARD L. ALLINGTON, PH.D., · AND KATHLEEN KRULL
ILLUSTRATED BY TOM GARCIA
Raintree Childrens Books • Milwaukee • Toronto • Melbourne • London

We are always thinking.
Have you ever wondered *why* we think?
This book will show you some of the reasons:

for fun

to figure out the best ways
of doing things

to make choices

to put things in order

to learn new things

to make sense out of things
that happen

As you read this story, tell what kind of thinking
is taking place on every page.

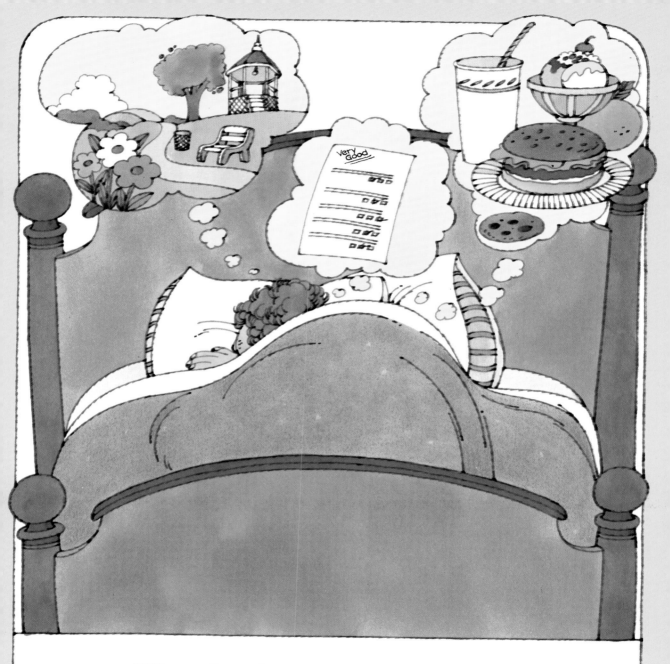

When I wake up, I think about all
the things that might happen that
day. I feel excited.

I think about getting dressed.
What should I put on first?
What should I put on last?

I fix breakfast.
What do I feel like having today?

I walk to school. I have to figure out
the fastest way of getting there.

Which way should I go?

At school, the teacher tells us to do
two things: "Draw a picture of yourself.
Then draw a picture of what you
want to be when you grow up."

First I think about all the things
I could be when I grow up.

Then I think about following
the teacher's directions.

The teacher puts some of the drawings
on the wall. I think about which
drawing I like the best.

cat
cow
dog
fish
bear

In reading class, we learn names for animals.
I have to remember all those words.

Which word goes with which animal?

In math class, we learn about adding.
I have to give the answers to the
problems. What are the answers?

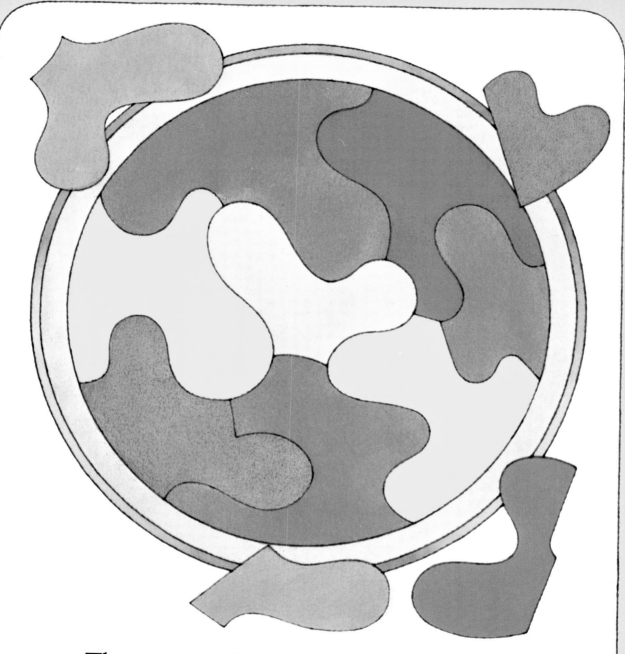

Then we work on puzzles.
Which piece is missing from the puzzle?

17

In science class, we look at pictures
of young and old animals.

Which are young? Which are old?

On the playground, we play hide-and-seek.
I think of a good hiding place.

How many people are playing
the game with me?

On the way home from school,
I think about things I see.

What is going to happen next?

I see things that have already happened.

What has happened?

After dinner, I clean my room.

What goes in the toy box?
What goes on the book shelf?
What goes in the closet?

Sometimes I watch TV. I think
about which show I want to watch.
Or should I turn the TV off?

Apple Treat

1. Wash apple.

2. Put a stick into the center.

3. Roll the apple in a bowl of honey until the apple is covered with honey.

4. Then sprinkle cereal or nuts on the apple.

I fix a snack. I follow
the directions very carefully.

When I go to bed, I think about things
that happened during the day.

I am still thinking — even in my sleep.

Can you think of a time when you are *not* thinking?
What words would you use to tell about it?

———————————————————

Make your own book about thinking.
Look at a newspaper or magazine.
Try to find pictures of people

thinking for fun

learning new things

remembering

having night dreams or daydreams

making choices

solving problems

following directions

Cut out the pictures.
Tape or paste them onto pieces of paper.
Fasten the papers together.
Tell someone what you think is happening in
each picture.
You may ask an adult to help you.